MARC BROWN

ARTHUR LOST AND FOUND

LB
1837

Little, Brown and Company
Boston New York Toronto London

For Sunny Macmillan,
with many thanks

First Edition

Adapted by Marc Brown from a teleplay by Kathy Waugh

Library of Congress Cataloging-in-Publication Data

Brown, Marc Tolon.
   Arthur lost and found / Marc Brown. — 1st ed.
      p.   cm.
   Summary: When Arthur and Buster try to take the bus to Arthur's
swimming lesson, they fall asleep and end up in a strange part of town.
   ISBN 0-316-10912-6
   [1. Aardvark — Fiction. 2. Buses — Fiction. 3. Lost children —
Fiction.] I. Title.
PZ7.B81618Anai 1998
[E] — dc21   97-46992

10 9 8 7 6 5 4 3 2 1

WOR

Published simultaneously in Canada by Little, Brown & Company
(Canada) Limited

Printed in the United States of America

"What are you supposed to be?" asked Arthur.
"I'm mashed potatoes," said D.W., "in the Festival of Foods at school tomorrow."

"Gee, too bad I have my swimming lesson," said Arthur.
"You'll have to take the bus to your lesson," said Mom,
"and I'll pick you up."
"All by myself?" asked Arthur.

"We've taken the bus before," said Mom. "You know how."

"Maybe I'll ask Buster to come along," said Arthur.

"Good idea," said Mom.

On the way to school, Arthur invited Buster.
"You mean the real bus?" asked Buster. "The one that goes all the way to the end of town?"
"Sure," said Arthur. "We just pay our money and go."

"I don't know," said Buster. "I heard about this guy who got on the bus, and it just kept going and going and going."

"We can study for our science test, and you can watch me swim," said Arthur. "It'll be fun."

After school, Arthur and Buster waited at the bus stop.
"Did you hear about the kid who didn't have enough
money?" asked Francine. "The driver wouldn't let him
off the bus."
All of a sudden Arthur didn't feel so well.
"Here comes the bus!" said Francine. "Good luck."

"Exact change only," growled the driver.
The boys paid him and quickly took their seats.
"Want to study for the test?" asked Arthur.
"Not really," said Buster.
Arthur took out his science book.
"'Chapter six,'" read Arthur. "'Habits of the Clam...'"

By the time the bus stopped at the pool, Arthur and Buster were sound asleep.

"Last stop," called the driver. "Everyone out!"

"Where are we?" asked Arthur.

"Who knows?" said Buster. "I think we passed the pool."

"I've never seen this part of town before," said Buster.
"We're lost!"
"Maybe we can find a police officer," said Arthur.

"Wait!" said Arthur. "There's a place with a phone!"

But the telephone had a sign on it.
"Sorry, it's been broken for weeks," said the man behind
the counter.

"I'm hungry," said Buster. "I always get hungry when I'm scared."

"No, you're just always hungry," said Arthur.

They bought six chocolate winkies and two cans of strawberry soda and thought about what to do next.

Meanwhile, back at home, the phone rang.
Arthur's little sister ran to answer it.
"Mom," D.W. yelled, "did we lose Arthur somewhere?"
"He's at his swimming lesson," said Mom. "In fact, it's almost time to pick him up. Who is it?"
"It's the man from the pool," said D.W. "Arthur isn't there."
"Give me the phone," gasped Mom. "What do you mean he's not there?"
"If Arthur's lost," said D.W., "can I have his room?"

Arthur and Buster finished their snacks. Then Arthur got an idea.

"Let's go back to the bus stop and try and get a bus home," said Arthur.

"Great idea!" said Buster. "Can you loan me some money for the bus? I spent all my money on winkies."

"Sure," said Arthur.

But when Arthur reached into his pocket, it was empty.

"Oh, no," said Arthur. "I spent all my money on strawberry sodas!"

"We're doomed," said Buster.

"Let's go to the bus stop anyway," said Arthur. "Maybe we can talk to the bus driver."

Arthur and Buster raced to the bus stop.
The bus was just pulling away.
"Oh, no!" said Arthur. "Wait! WAIT!" he called.
The bus squealed to a stop.

"Whaddaya kids want?" asked the driver.

"We're lost," Arthur explained. "We were supposed to get off at the pool, but we fell asleep and then we spent all our money on winkies. Now we can't get home, and I'm really sorry."

"Hey, kids," said the driver, "I've heard enough. Happens all the time."

"Really?" asked Arthur.

"Hop on," said the driver. "By the way, my name's Sam."
"I'm Arthur. He's Buster."
"Let's make a quick stop and give your folks a call," said
Sam. "Just in case they're getting a little nervous."
"Great idea," said Arthur.

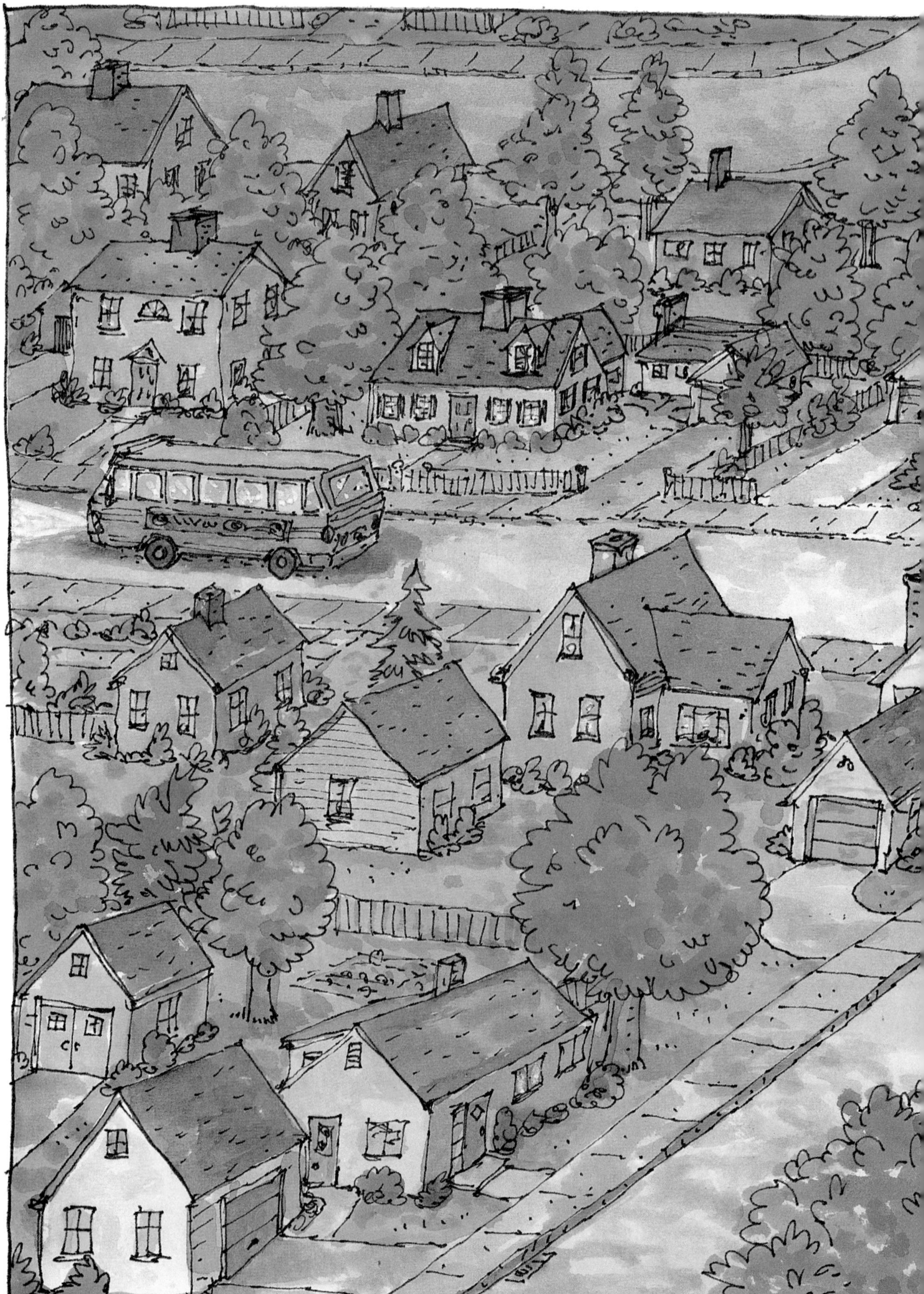

Sam stopped the bus right in front of
Arthur's house instead of at the corner.
"Thanks, Sam," said Arthur and Buster.
"See ya 'round," said Sam.
Everyone on the bus waved good-bye.

When Arthur opened the door, his family ran to give him kisses and hugs.

D.W. was so happy that she hugged Buster, too.

"No kisses, please," said Buster.

Arthur told his family everything that had happened.

"I liked the part where you were lost best," said D.W.
"That's when I had a new bedroom."
Then Dad gave Buster a ride home.

That night, when both Mom and Dad tucked Arthur
into bed, he was very sleepy.
"You were smart to figure out what to do," said Mom.
"We're very proud of you," said Dad.
They kissed Arthur good night and turned off the light.

Suddenly, the door burst open and the light went on.
"What's going on?" said Arthur.
"I'm making sure you're not lost again," said D.W.
"Good brothers are hard to find."
Arthur yawned. "So are good sisters.
Good night, D.W."